The Time Detectives

Terry Deary trained as an actor before turning to writing full time. He has many successful fiction and non-fiction children's books to his name, and is rarely out of the bestseller charts.

Other titles in the series:

The Witch of Nightmare Avenue
The Pirates of the Dark Park
King Arthur's Bones

The Time Detectives

Book 3

The Princes in Terror Tower

TERRY DEARY

Illustrated by Martin Remphry

faber and faber

To Frank Gray

First published in 2000
by Faber and Faber Limited
3 Queen Square London WCIN 3AU

Origination: Miles Kelly Publishing
Printed in Italy

A CIP record for this book
is available from the British Library

ISBN 0-571-20117-2

Contents

The Time Detectives
All about us

These are the files of the toughest team ever to tackle time-crime. We solve mysteries of the past, at last – and fast.

We are the Time Detectives.

My name is Bucket.

Katie Bucket. Commander of the Time Detectives.

And here is my squad. I wrote the secret files myself so you know they're true. Trust me...

Number: TD 001

Name:

Katie Bucket

Appearance:

Gorgeous, beautiful and smart. The slightly scruffy clothes and messy hair are just a disguise to fool the enemy.

Report:

Katie Bucket is the boss,
Grown-ups always make her cross.
She's the Time Detectives' leader.
Cos she's brainy they all need her!

Special skills:

Cunning, brave, quick-thinking. Really I'm too modest to tell you just how great I am.

Hobbies:

Playing football, wrestling snakes, making trouble. (It's a full-time hobby just being so popular!)

Favourite victim:

Miss Toon our teacher.

Catch-phrase:

"Trust me, I know what I'm doing."

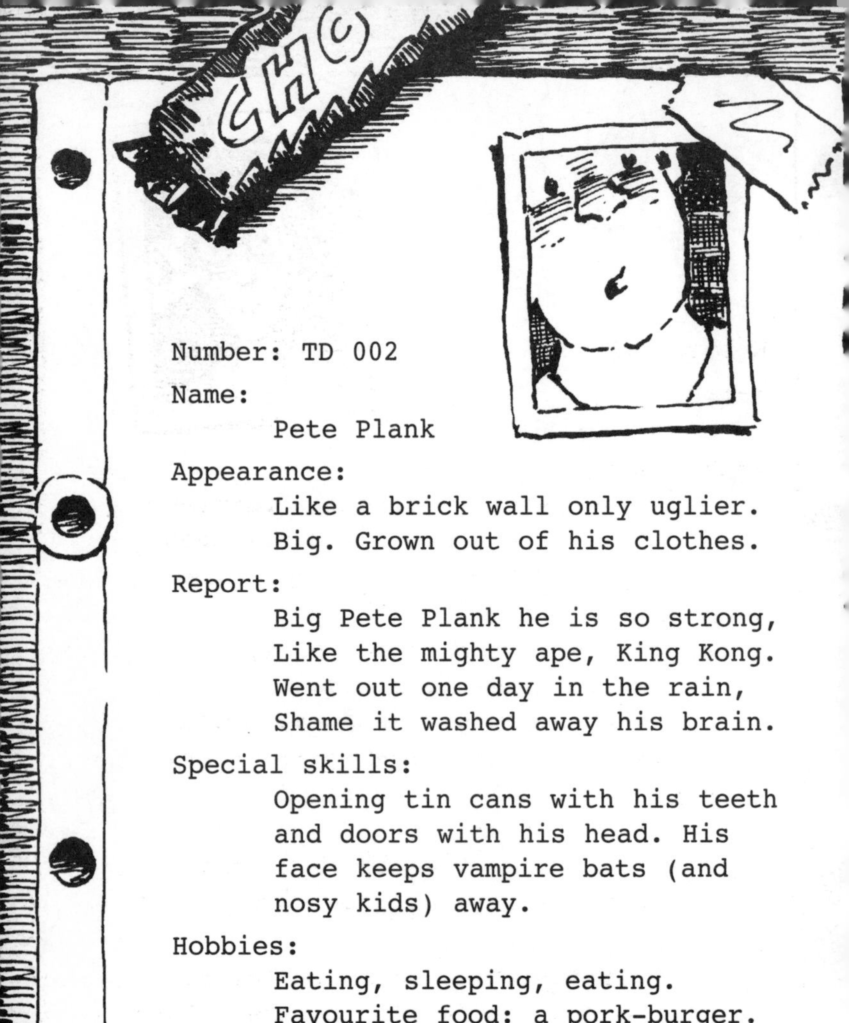

Number: TD 002

Name:

Pete Plank

Appearance:

Like a brick wall only uglier.
Big. Grown out of his clothes.

Report:

Big Pete Plank he is so strong,
Like the mighty ape, King Kong.
Went out one day in the rain,
Shame it washed away his brain.

Special skills:

Opening tin cans with his teeth and doors with his head. His face keeps vampire bats (and nosy kids) away.

Hobbies:

Eating, sleeping, eating.
Favourite food: a pork-burger. (That's a pig in a bun, you understand.)

Catch-phrase:

"Uhh?"

Number: TD 003

Name:

Gary Grint

Appearance:

A weed with spectacles. Carries more gadgets in his anorak than a moon rocket.

Report:

Gary Grint, computer whiz,
Internetting is his biz.
Knows so much he's awful boring,
Talks till everyone is snoring.

Special skills:

Electronic gadgets, cracking codes, squeezing through small spaces – like letter-boxes.

Hobbies:

Train-spotting, chess, playing the violin (favourite tune: 'The dying cat').

Catch-phrase:

"I'll bet you didn't know this!"

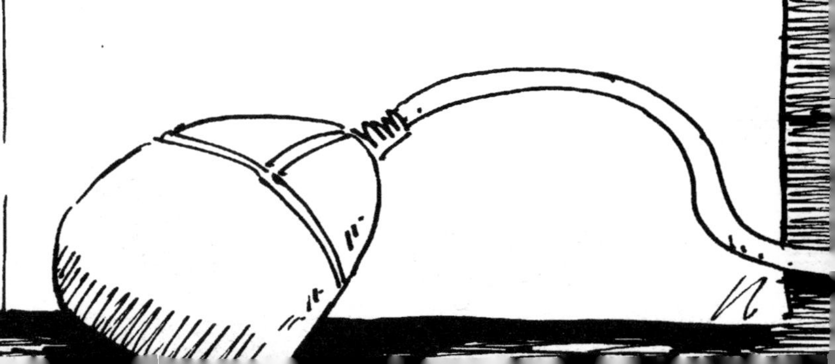

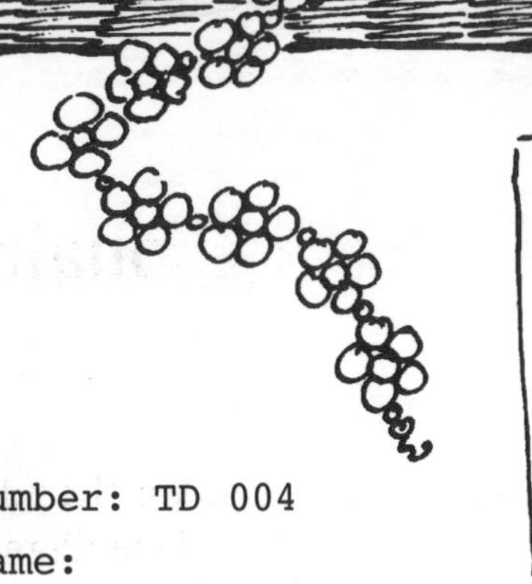

Number: TD 004

Name:

Mabel Tweed

Appearance:

So squeaky clean you could eat your dinner off her shining shoes. She's all posh frocks and white socks.

Report:

Mabel Tweed is so good,
So polite and sweet as pud.
Does her homework neat and quick,
Teacher's pet. She makes me sick!

Special skills:

Creeping, grovelling and being smarmy. I only let the lucky kid join TDs cos her dad's a millionaire.

Hobbies:

Tidying her room, polishing her bike, running errands for adults. Favourite place: at Miss Toon's feet.

Catch-phrase:

"Do excuse me."

Chapter 1
Missing Mabel the millionaire

It all started in Miss Toon's history lesson that dull Tuesday morning. (It was as dull as Pete Plank's brain.)

"This term we study the Tudors in history. So, we'll begin today with the way the first Tudor came to the throne... and the mystery of the Princes in the Tower!" our toothy teacher twittered.

When we heard the word 'mystery' the Time Detectives sat up... all except Pete Plank, who was asleep at the time.

"Mystery, Miss?" Gary Grint grinned. "What happened to them?"

Miss Toon whispered, "That's the mystery! No... one... knows!"

And so then we were as hopelessly hooked as a haddock. I could see it! Adventure, excitement... and a day off school! "So tell us!" I ordered the twittering teacher.

She obeyed me, of course. Want to know what she said? Then read on...

"It was the end of the Middle Ages... now, you all know what the Middle Ages are... yes, Katie," She said, as my hand shot up.

"Please Miss, my dad's 35 and he's in his middle ages," I told her.

Miss Toon (who must be at least 30 herself) looked a bit pained. "No, Katie Bucket. People over 35 may be middle-aged... to someone as young as you. But historians call the time from the Normans to the Tudors the Middle Ages."

"I knew that," I muttered to Pete next to me and woke him up.

"Uhh?" he grunted.

While Miss Toon nattered about Normans I read the morning newspaper under the desk...

The Duckpool Daily News

3 January 55p

MISERY OF MISSING MABEL'S MUM

By our Staff Reporter

Missing: Mabel Tweed, aged 9.

MABEL TWEED, daughter of Mayor Walter Tweed, is still missing after vanishing on a New Year trip to London. The girl, a pupil in Miss Toon's class at Duckpool Primary, was invited to spend New Year's Eve on a River Thames boat-trip by her mother, Henrietta (41) and her stepfather-to-be Ricky T Hurd (29).

The trip was to have ended with a party in the Tower of London. Mabel was last seen on the boat shortly before it reached the Tower. Her mother fears she may have slipped and fallen overboard. "I never heard a splash," she sniffed into her expensive silk handkerchief, "but we were all singing Auld Lang Syne so loud we wouldn't have heard her."

Mayor Tweed said today, "Typical. That stupid woman would lose her head if it wasn't bolted on. Mabel is my pride and joy – and the heir to my millions – cos I'm a millionaire, you know. We will leave no stone unturned and no river undredged until we find my darling girl. Chief Inspector Norse of Duckpool police is on the case."

The missing girl's stepfather-to-be, Ricky T Hurd, said, "I loved that girl like my own daughter – well, like my own stepdaughter – which she was about to become – and which is why I loved her like my own stepdaughter. I am quite sure she'll turn up. She was a very strong swimmer. Luckily it was a freezing cold night – far too cold for sharks to get her and chew her legs off."

Chief Inspector Norse of Duckpool CID, who is helping Scotland Yard, said last night, "I am quite sure we will find little Mabel, dead or alive, and return her to the loving arms of her parents – all three of them."

MISSING FOR NINE WEEKS

CAT RETURNS

"Mabel's still missing," I whispered to Pete.

"Missing what? Missing school?" he asked. "Is that why she's not in her seat?"

"No! Missing-missing... gone missing, I mean. Remember? We said a prayer for her this morning in school assembly?" I reminded him.

"Thought that was for a girl called Mavis Weed?" he frowned.

"Yeah," I sighed. Our headteacher, Mr 'Potty' Potterton, managed to get her name wrong. I was going to explain but Miss Toon was glaring at me. Her mouth was tight as a nun's who just sucked a lemon. "Yes, Miss," I said brightly, guessing she'd just asked me a question... like, "Are you listening Katie Bucket?"

She nodded, "Good. Then I'll show you something called a 'family tree'," and she unrolled a coloured chart I guess she'd spent the Christmas holiday drawing. Sad lady. "Do you know what a family tree is, Pete?" she asked.

Pete frowned. “We’ve got a tree outside our house my mum calls our family’s tree. She used to make Dad sweep the leaves up every autumn – until he had a nasty accident.”

“What happened?” Gary asked.

“One day Dad was sweeping the leaves and he fell out of the tree,” Pete explained.

Gary had no answer to that, so he made it, “—”

“No, Pete. A family tree is a chart that shows the names of the people in a family and the way they’re linked together. Look... here are the last of the Plantagenet kings of the Middle Ages,” she said, and showed us the chart...

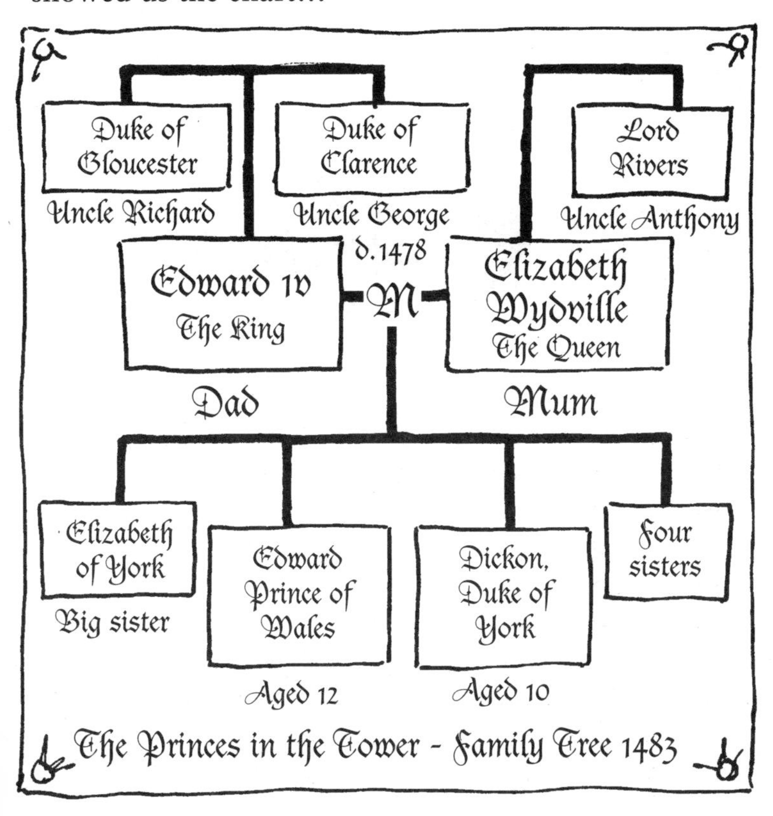

"You see? It's simple!" Miss Toon said happily. "Elizabeth married King Edward IV. They had two sons, little Edward and Dickon. Whenever a king dies then his eldest son is the next king. Who would get the throne when Edward IV died, Gloria?" she asked Gloria Green.

"Please, Miss, Edward Prince of Wales!" Gloria said and looked smug. I don't know why. It was an easy question.

"Now, Gary Grint, I want you to read about the death of Edward IV from page 112 of your book, *The Magical Middle Ages*," the teacher said.

Gary sniffed. This was all simple stuff. He was like me and wanted to get to the exciting mystery bit. He read quickly...

Now King Edward IV was a fine figure of a man, tall and handsome. Sadly he was also a disgusting and greedy man. In fact, he was so greedy he would enjoy a huge feast, then he would drink a special medicine. The medicine made him so sick that he threw up all that he'd eaten. When his stomach was empty he could start feasting and fill it up again.

Of course, all this pigging and vomiting weakened his strong body. He grew fat and feeble. One day he was out boating on the River Thames when he caught a chill. The chill turned to a fever and the fever killed him.

His family were surprised at his sudden death and no-one was quite ready to take the throne.

"Thank you, Gary," Miss Toon smiled. "Now, look at the family tree," she went on, pointing to her chart that she'd pinned to the blackboard. "Who took dead Ed's crown?" Suddenly she pointed at Pete Plank. "Peter! Who took Edward's crown?"

Pete, who'd been daydreaming, jumped and looked worried and guilty. "Uhh?"

"I asked you who took Edward's crown?"

"Please, Miss," he gasped, "it wasn't me!"

Chapter 2
The Tower trip test

"Awwww! Miss!" I moaned. "We aren't going to find out about the Princes in the Tower this way, are we?"

The teacher looked at me carefully. "How would you like to do it, Katie?" she asked.

"Well, I think we have to go to the Tower of London and investigate for ourselves," I told her.

"Get a feel for the place, Katie?" she suggested.

"Get a feel for the place, Miss," I agreed.

"Get into the shoes of the characters, Katie?"

"Get into the shoes of the characters, Miss!"

"Get a day off school, Katie?"

"Get a day off… errrr. We'd be terribly sad to miss school, of course," I lied.

She tapped her teeth with her felt-tip pen while she thought about it. "You need some more facts before you go. You need to know what you're looking for. Spend today doing research and I'll ask Mr Potterton if you can go tomorrow."

Gary Grint leaned across the table and hissed, "This all happened five hundred years ago. We can find out all we want to know from books and computers. We won't find anything new by going to the Tower of London!"

"Maybe we'll find nothing new about these boring old princes – but we may find something new about Mabel Tweed!" I told him.

Slowly his worried frown cleared. "Oh! I see!" he nodded.

"I just hope tomorrow isn't going to be too late," I said grimly.

That morning break-time it was sleeting outside, and none of our wimpy teachers wanted to do a playground duty, so we spent the time indoors. Gary switched on the classroom television and a news-flash shocked us...

"Sad about Mabel," Pete said.

"Yeah. The tears are running down my legs, Pete," I said. Mabel was a snob and a pain in the neck. I just didn't believe she had drowned or disappeared off the face of the Thames.

Miss Toon swept into the room after break and rapped her family tree. "Now, you've a lot to learn, you Time Detectives, if you're off to the Tower of London tomorrow."

"Potty Potterton says we can go?" Pete cried.

"Mr Potterton said that he would take you!" our teacher said sternly.

We groaned.

"But you have to be experts in the mystery of the princes before you go," she explained. "He'll give you a test after school tonight."

We groaned again. Schools can be prisons at times.

"Does he have to come?" Gary asked.

Miss Toon glared at him. "After what happened to poor Mabel you should know you have to have an adult with you."

"And she had a boat-load of adults with her," Gary grumbled.

Miss Toon raised a hand. "Shall we get on with the lesson?"

"Of course, Miss Toon! We'll be thrilled to have Mr Potterton with us!" I agreed. Gary opened his mouth to argue but I whispered to him, "Trust me, I know what I'm doing!"

"Right!" the teacher said. (Have you noticed how many times teachers say that word 'right'? I counted one hundred and fifty three in one day!) "Edward IV died in 1483. Can you see a problem they may have had?"

"Yeah!" Pete said. Everyone turned towards him. Pete never knew the answer to anything. "They couldn't find a coffin big enough for his fat body!"

"I think they'd have made an extra-large one specially for him, Pete," Miss Toon said. "I meant, can you see the problem for the English people? Young Prince Edward was the dead king's oldest son – he would be crowned king. But why was that a bit of a problem?"

And that's another thing about teachers. They ask questions all the time. They know the answers – so why don't they just tell us?

Gloria Green put her grubby little hand in the air. "Please, Miss Toon, Prince Edward was only twelve years old. England would have a kid for a king!"

"Well done, Gloria!" Miss Toon smiled.

"I knew that," I told Gloria, "little Miss Smarty-knickers!"

"The king needed someone called a 'Protector' to help him until he was old enough to rule by himself. Look at the family tree. Who do you think should be his protector?"

Interesting question. I guessed this Protector would be as powerful as the king himself!

"I'd pick Elizabeth Wydville, his mum," I decided.

"In the Middle Ages women weren't thought fit to rule England," Miss Toon sighed.

"Then the dead king's brother should get the job. That Duke of Clarence!" Gary Grint suggested.

Miss Toon nodded. "You see 'd. 1478' under his name? That means he died in 1478. He'd caused trouble for King Edward so he'd been executed."

"The king had his own brother executed?" I asked.

"That's right. Some monks wrote a history of the time... look at what they said," the teacher told us and projected a picture of an old document onto the white wall of the classroom...

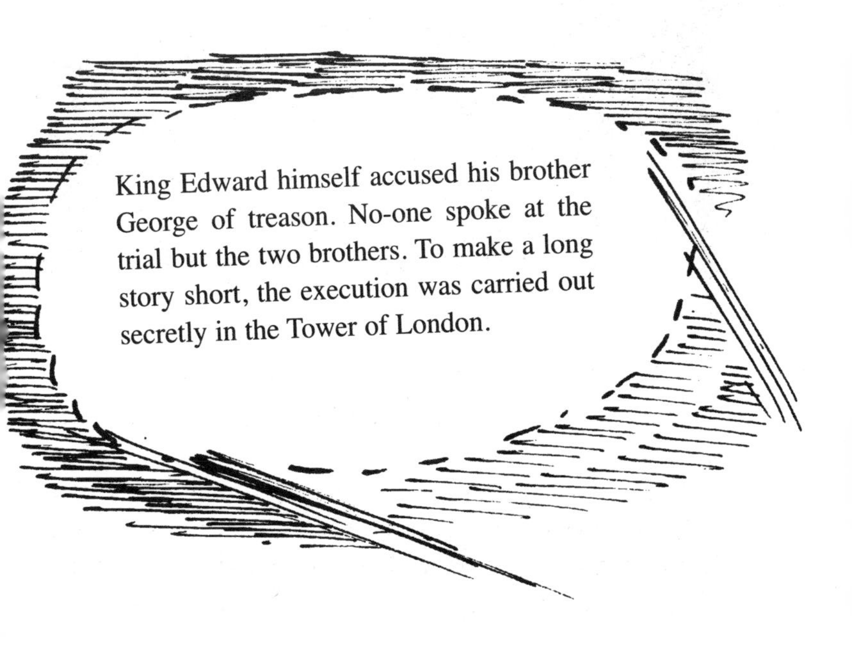

King Edward himself accused his brother George of treason. No-one spoke at the trial but the two brothers. To make a long story short, the execution was carried out secretly in the Tower of London.

"Now, the curious and gruesome thing is," said Miss Toon, shifting the paper, "the way George died. Here's a piece from a book written by a visitor to London, Dominic Mancini...

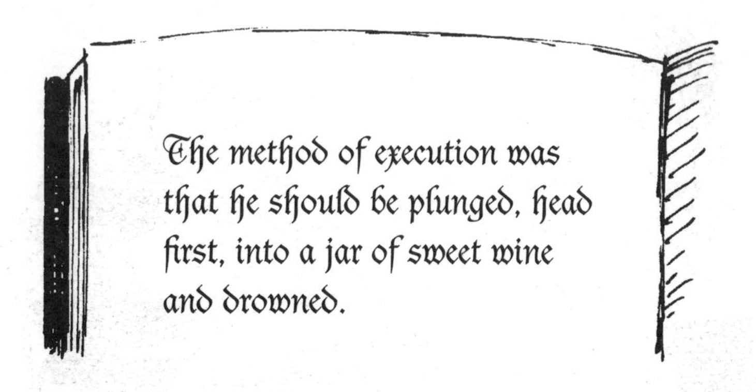
The method of execution was that he should be plunged, head first, into a jar of sweet wine and drowned.

"Some people think George asked to be executed that way! But, most horrible of all, many people think the king's younger brother, Richard, did the drowning!" Miss Toon said.

"Didn't he mind?" Pete asked.

Miss Toon gave a secret smile and answered, "Well, if he did mind, he didn't whine about it!"

Why are teachers' jokes always so dreadful?

Chapter 3
A truly terrible Tower tale

We had lunch. The school cook had made her usual delicious stew of dead hedgehogs she'd scraped up from the road.

The lunch-time news had nothing new on Mabel but an important clue to her disappearance. Being the leader of the Time Detectives I spotted the clue, of course, but Pete and Gary missed it...

"He's a Beefeater!" I told Pete.

The big blockhead blinked, and said, "My dad's a pizza-eater."

"He works at the Tower," I said.

"So what?" Gary frowned.

"So... that's where Mabel went missing! Suspicious!" I told him.

"And that's where the princes went missing. Are you going to suspect him of that as well?" Gary sneered.

"Shut up, Gary," I said. He can be very annoying.

"He seems pretty sure she's gone for good," I said, snapping off the radio.

Gary shook his head. "If she fell in the Thames on a freezing night then she's dead of cold if she hasn't been found by now," he said sadly.

"What's the Traitor's Gate?" Pete asked. Pete always asked good questions. He didn't have any good answers but he always had good questions.

I looked at one of the books we were studying and found a plan of the Tower. "See, the Tower is on the bank of the river. Most people go in through the front gate. But traitors were brought by boat, landed at these steps and taken in the back door."

Pete pulled a face. "Even if Mabel did swim to the Traitor's Gate she wouldn't get in. No-one's going to leave the back door to the Tower open so thieves can walk in and nick the crown jewels, are they?"

"No, Pete," I sighed. "But I'm sure the answer lies there somewhere. We have to go to the Tower."

"Tomorrow with Potty."

"Only if we pass his test," I said. "Let's get on with it."

Then we set about studying the tale of the Princes in the Tower so 'Potty' Potterton could test us. By half past three we had all the information we needed.

Have you noticed how teachers like to tell you stories? That's because simple little minds find it easy to listen to stories. No-one is simpler than Potty Potterton, so we turned the princes' tale into a story.

When the class had gone home into the freezing sleet we sat our headteacher in Miss Toon's seat and asked, "Are you sitting comfortably?"

"Yes," he nodded like one of those little dogs some sad people put on the back shelf of their cars.

"Then we'll begin..."

The mystery of the terrible Tower

Once upon a time there were two little princes of England, Prince Edward and Prince Dickon. Now Prince Edward lived in Wales with his kind Uncle Anthony who taught him all about being a king. Little Prince Dickon lived in London with his mum, the queen, and played so happily with his five sweet sisters.

Then, one sad day, the old king died. "Boo-hoo!" the queen and her daughters sobbed. "Booey-hooey!" went little Dickon too.

And "Oh, I say! That means that now I'm king!" said young Prince Edward.

So kind Uncle Anthony took poor Prince Edward off to London, there to meet his mum and his small brother (Dickon) and be crowned.

But after a few days upon the road they stopped at a small town called Stony Stratford. And who should they meet there but Edward's wicked Uncle Richard. "Hello, dear little Edward," wicked Uncle Richard said. "I've come to take you to safe to London."

"Thank you, Uncle Richard," brave Prince Edward said politely. "But Uncle Anthony is looking after me. He's my mummy's brother, did you know?"

"And I'm your daddy's brother, did you know. Alas, your Uncle Anthony's an evil man and so is your mischievous mummy!" Uncle Richard told the boy. "They planned to rule the country and to make themselves quite filthy rich! So I have come to rescue you."

"Where is dear Uncle Anthony?" the worried Edward asked.

"I've locked him safe away in my great castle up in Yorkshire. When he's quite forgotten I will have his hapless head hacked off!" the wicked Uncle Richard said.

So Prince Edward and his wicked Uncle Richard rode on into London. And there, beside the River Thames, stood the mighty Tower of London. "Your mummy still has nasty friends," the wicked Uncle Richard told the prince.

"You'll lock them in this Tower and keep them in?" Prince Edward asked.

"No, no, my boy. I'll lock you in and keep them out!" his uncle chuckled. So the prince was locked up in the grey and gloomy Tower where black ravens croaked and flapped above the mighty walls.

Then Uncle Richard went along the river to the palace where the queen and her young Dickon stayed. "Let me in, dear Queen," cruel Richard said. "Or send dear Dickon out to me."

"No! No!" the crying queen called back.

"Then I will have my soldiers batter at your door and beat upon your walls until they tumble to the ground!" the wicked uncle laughed.

"Alas, alack, and woe is me!" the woeful woman wailed. And then she sent her little son outside to where his Uncle Richard waited.

"Hello, dear nephew," Richard cackled. "Come with me and I will take you somewhere safe, my child. I'll take you where your brother Edward waits for you. And you two princes can play all day and have such happy times!"

And so the princes ended up in the mighty Tower. And, do you know, the little lads were never seen alive again!

Where do you think Prince Edward and young Dickon went? And did they live or did they die? And if they died then who would kill such helpless boys?

That's the mystery of the terrible Tower!

Potty Potterton took out his handkerchief and blew his thin and pointed nose. "What a sad story! What's the answer? What did happen to them? I hope they lived happily ever after!"

"That's the trouble," I said, patting his hand because I could see he was upset. "No-one knows. But if we go off to the Tower of London we may find the clues and solve the mystery! See?"

He brightened up. "I'll organise a trip," he said. "Send out forms for parents to fill in, arrange insurance, book the bus, book a tour of the Tower, get money from the school fund..."

"All before tomorrow morning?" Pete gasped.

Potty's bushy eyebrows flew up. "Tomorrow morning! Good grief, no! It'll take at least a month!"

I looked at the Time Detectives team. "Mabel will definitely be dead by then," I said grimly and they nodded.

"Mabel?" Potty said. "Was one of the princes called Mabel?"

"Never mind," I sighed. "Never mind."

Chapter 4
Crystal on the conk

The Time Detectives were gloomy as we walked home through the damp and slushy streets.

"Mabel was never really one of us," I said.

"Not really," Gary agreed.

"She just stuck her nose in and tagged along," I said. "She wasn't a lot of help in solving mysteries."

"Not really... well, her money sometimes came in handy!" Pete said.

I slithered to a stop. "Money! That's all we need!" I cried. "We don't need Potty Potterton and his school trip. We just need to take a trip to the Tower ourselves! What's stopping us?"

"Money," Pete said. "We haven't got any. We're not millionaires."

"No... but Mayor Walter Tweed is! Mabel's dad may give us the money to try and find his daughter! Let's go!"

"Where to?" Pete asked.

"To the Town Hall! He's always there."

We hurried through the wet streets and raced into the High Street. Long before we reached the Town Hall I knew we were too late. There were dazzling flashes of blue lights as police cars, fire-engines and ambulances blocked the road and crowds of people gathered to watch – they always do.

A television reporter was standing at the bottom of the Town Hall steps and talking to a camera while people with half a brain moved behind him and tried to get into the picture. I pulled Pete away and made him listen to the reporter. He told us all we needed to know…

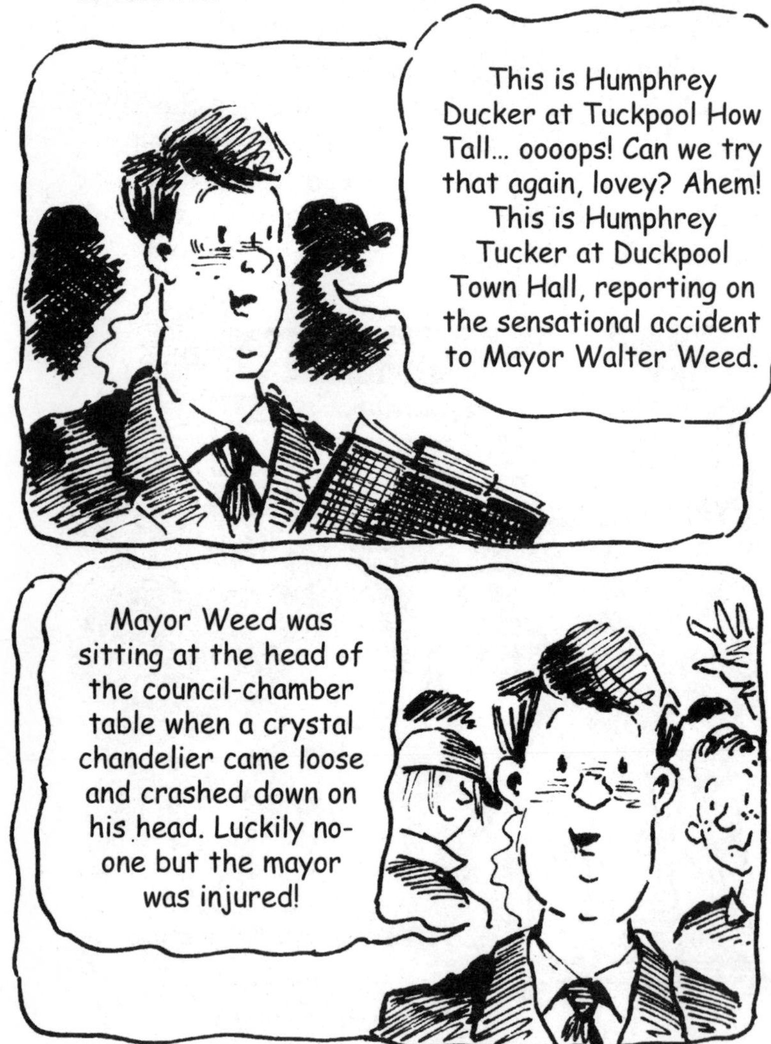

I have here Sergeant Horse of Duckpool police
It's Chief Inspector, actually. And the name is Norse.
Whatever - Tell me, Constable Coarse, is foul play suspected?
Foul play is indeed suspected. The chandelier chain had been replaced by a rope which was then sprinkled with grated cheese. Rats were then set free to nibble at the cheese and thus chewed through the rope!

Why would a killer go to all that trouble?
So he or she could be miles away when the chandelier fell. It could be anyone... it could be you!
But I'm not miles away! I'm here! Anyway, how is Mayor Walter Weed?
It's Tweed actually.

Sorry – how is Mayor Tweed Weed?
HELLO MUM
Very poorly – and the chandelier's even worse. Totally wrecked! But we'll give up the search for his lost daughter and find this dangerous lunatic instead!

Thank you. This is Tumphrey Ducker at Pucktool Foul Wall returning you to the studio!
HELL
DUCKPOOL F.C.

As the television lights faded out we turned to see Mayor Tweed carried down the steps on a stretcher, bits of chandelier still wrapped around his scrawny neck and firemen wrestling with it. He disappeared into the ambulance, sirens blared and the crowds began to drift off home to watch it all over again on television.

One car was left outside the Town Hall on the double yellow lines. It was a silver Rolls Royce with a personal number plate that spelled out the mayor's initials – T for Tweed, W for Walter, and the number one-T. "Look! TW1T!" I told Pete and Gary.

"Here! Watch who you're calling a twit!" Pete scowled.

"The mayor's car! That's what we need!" I said and led the way across to the driver. He was watching a small television, set into the dashboard.

"Ah, my good man!" I said in the nearest voice to Mabel's I could manage. "Mayor Tweed is unwell."

The driver was a young man in a peaked cap and a green uniform. He twisted his lip and nose in a comic mask. "Unwell? Un-well!! He's half-dead, poor old weedy Tweed!"

"Yes," I nodded, "But, before he had an argument with that chandelier, he ordered us to go to the Tower of London to track down his lost daughter. He told us to go in this car," I lied.

"Fair enough. Hop in," the driver said. "I speed to the needs of Tweed! That's my motto! I've got it written on my dashboard!"

Gary and Pete looked dazed but they stepped into the car and sat down on the huge back seat. They stared at the computer, the television, the fridge full of cans of coke and the telephone. "Amazing!" Gary said, switching on the computer.

"Nah! Cheap car!" I jeered. "Hasn't even got a snooker table."

We moved off swiftly, the only sound the hiss of the fat tyres through the slush. We headed out of Duckpool onto the London road.

"Here! I'll bet you didn't know this!" Gary said. "This computer's connected to the internet. Look what I've found out about the Princes in the Tower! It was written by that Mancini man."

We put our heads close to the screen and began to read what was written on it...

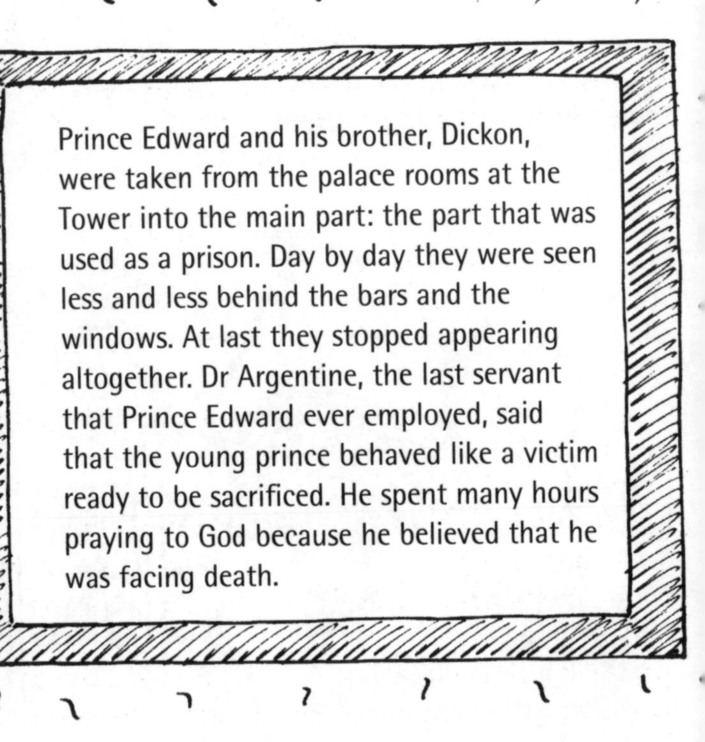

"It looks bad for the princes," I agreed. "But, like that Mancini man says, he's not sure that they were killed or how it was done. And we don't know who did it. There's still a lot of Time Detective work to be done."

"And you can't believe that Dr Argentine anyway!" Gary told me.

"Why not?"

"Because he'd just been given the sack when he said that. He must have been angry – probably trying to stir up trouble."

Pete looked out of the window at the cars rushing past. "It's funny, you know. The princes lost their Uncle Anthony and then they disappeared. It's a bit like Mabel and her dad."

"Eh?" Gary grunted.

But I understood. "Pete! That's brilliant! The two things were linked. One had to happen so the other could happen! Mayor Walter Tweed's accident and Mabel's disappearance were linked!"

Gary squinted at me. "OK, Miss Clever-clogs. How?"

I sniffed. "If I knew that I'd know who took Mabel and why; who attacked the mayor and why."

"But you don't know," Gary said.

"Not yet," I told him. "But I will find out… even if it kills you."

Chapter 5
Really rotten Richard

"Why would anyone want to hurt Mabel?" Gary asked.

"I often feel like strangling her myself," I told him. "She can be very annoying."

He sighed. "That's true. Maybe she upset someone on the river-boat and they threw her over the side!"

I shook my head. "Mabel's disappearance has something to do with Mayor Tweed's accident. We should be asking, why would anyone want to hurt Mayor Tweed?"

The driver looked over his shoulder. The glass screen was open and his ears had been flapping. "If you ask me," he said, "if you ask me they were after his money!"

That made sense. "So," I said slowly, "who would get Mayor Tweed's money if he died?"

"Mabel," the driver said. "Often heard him talk about it."

"Mabel tried to kill her dad?" Pete asked, trying to work it out.

"No, I don't think so," Gary said. "Mayor Tweed was supposed to die under a rat-nibbled chandelier. Mabel would become a millionaire..."

"But Mabel is too young to spend millions," I said. "They wouldn't let her. She'd have to have a guardian."

Gary was jumping with excitement. "Just like Prince Edward in the Tower – he had a guardian – a Protector! Whoever controlled the prince controlled the country! Whoever controls Mabel controls the millions!"

"Yeah, Gary, but the prince was probably bumped off."

"I know! And as soon as Mabel gets the money then she'll be bumped off. Don't you see?"

I saw – and it wasn't a pretty picture. "Mayor Tweed has to die first – like King Edward IV had to die first. As soon as he's dead then Mabel's finished."

The driver had switched on the radio and we listened for the latest report...

...And with the time at five o'clock we take you over to the newsroom for the six o'clock news on Duckpool FM.
Here in Duckpool this afternoon a daring attempt was made on the life of millionaire mayor, Walter Tweed. Mayor Tweed is recovering in hospital where he made the following statement...
"Gurgle, gurgle – me sit at table and light goes boppy-bop on me head! Hee! Hee! Ouch! Hurty me little head!"
Mayor Tweed is expected to make a full recovery. Police have taken the police guard away from his door because the mayor said, "Me no like men with pointy heads and shiny buttons. Me got teddy to look after me!"
Chief Inspector Norse said the mayor should be safe. They don't have chandeliers or rats in Duckpool Hospital.
And now with news of the Duckpool seagulls that have reached the finals of the synchronised swimming championships, here is our water-sports reporter Ivor Quacker...

The driver switched off the radio and yawned. "I wish you wouldn't do that at ninety miles an hour," I told him.

"I speed to the needs of Tweed!" he shrugged. "Looks like your friend Mabel is safe as long as the mayor recovers," he said.

I picked up the car telephone and got through to Duckpool Police Station. "Tell Inspector Norse to guard Mayor Tweed night and day! Someone has tried to kill him once. They will try again!"

"Who shall I say is calling?" the man on the other end asked.

"A friend," I said and put the phone down quickly.

The car swished on through the damp night and I leaned closer to my Time Detectives so the nosy driver couldn't hear. "Solve the mystery of the Princes in the Tower and we solve the mystery of Mabel and the mayor."

Gary tapped away at the computer while I tried to explain to Pete.

"The princes were sent to the Tower of London. At first they stayed in the palace. But then they were taken into the prison part. We need to know what happened to them next."

Gary tried to sort out the reports for us and put them in some sort of order...

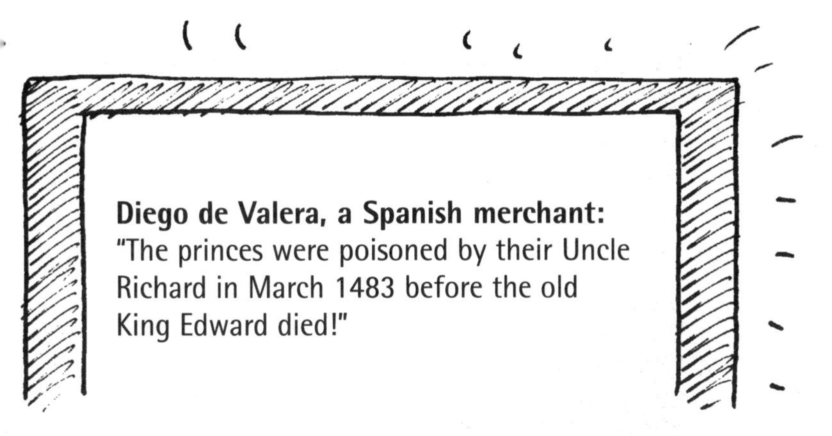

"That's nonsense!" I said.

"But it shows how people gossiped about the princes," Gary muttered.

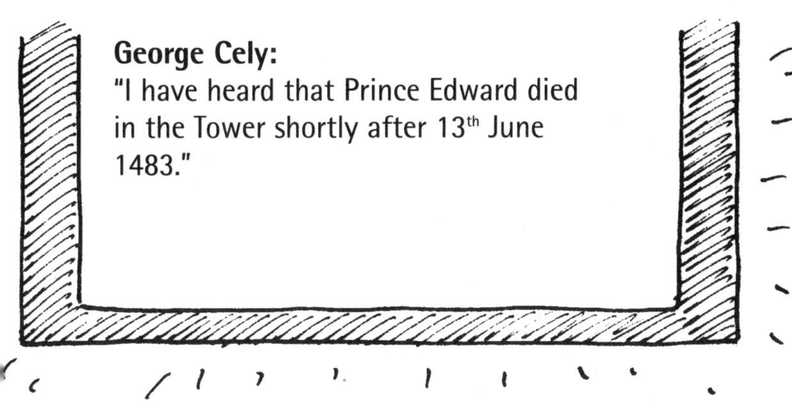

"So the princes were dead before their Uncle Richard was crowned king!"

"Rubbish," Gary snorted. "Little Prince Dickon was still with his mother when Uncle Richard took him to the Tower on 16th June!"

The Crowland Chronicle:
"There were rumours in September 1483 that the princes had met their fate by some unknown manner of destruction."

"That's more like it!" I said. "Uncle Richard locked up the princes in the middle of June, had himself crowned in July and the princes were bumped off in September!"

"Yes," Gary agreed. He showed me the other facts he'd found on the internet...

Robert Ricard, recorder of Bristol:
"In this year ending 15 September 1483 the two sons of King Edward IV were put to silence in the Tower."

R F Green, Historical Notes:
"The princes were put to death in the Tower before the end of the mayor's year, November 1483."

The Great Chronicle:
"The children were seen playing in the garden of the tower a few times before November, then no more."

"So most people believed that Uncle Richard took the crown in July and the princes were killed around September?" I said.

"Uhh?" Pete said. "But who did it?"

Gary pointed to his screen. "There's one main suspect..."

John Rous:
"The princes' Uncle Richard met Prince Edward at Stony Stratford on 30 April 1483. He met the prince with kisses and hugs, but within three months he had killed him, along with his little brother Dickon."

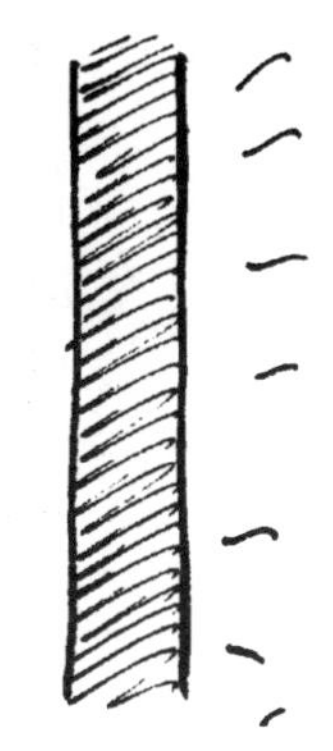

"So Uncle Richard locked the princes up in May, stole Prince Edward's crown in June, had himself made king in July and then had the boys murdered," I said.

"That doesn't help us to find Mabel," he sighed.

"Maybe it does," I said.

"And Mabel it doesn't," Gary grinned.

It wasn't that funny.

"Our first job when we get to the Tower is to find out more about wicked Uncle Richard!"

Chapter 6
The killer king

When we reached the Tower of London it looked very pretty, glowing in the floodlights. We left the driver to park and told him to wait. "I speed to the needs of Tweed!" he said.

"No. Don't speed anywhere. Stay here till you're told to leave," I said.

"I speed to the needs of Tweed!" he repeated. "And if that means staying here then here I stay."

"That driver's a few yo-yos short of a toyshop," Gary muttered as we walked across the moat and through the first of the massive gates.

The princes wouldn't have had floodlights, I thought, as we walked through the entrance. Just dark, damp walls, running rats... not to mention the ghastly ghosts of all the people who'd died there.

A man in a red uniform with golden trim stood in front of us. "We're just about to close for the day," he said. "Hardly worth paying to get in."

"Are you a Beefeater?" Gary asked.

"I am, young sir," the man said proudly.

"My dad's a pizza-eater," Pete said, just as proudly.

The man in red looked baffled. Pete has that effect on people. I said quickly, "Good evening, my good man. As you can see from the car, we represent Mayor Tweed of Duckpool. We've been sent here to investigate the disappearance of his daughter!"

The man nodded. "You'll want to talk to her Uncle Ricky, then. Hang about and I'll go and find him," he offered.

"You are too kind," I said. "I will mention your good work the next time I see the Queen!"

The man's red face split into a grin. "Thank you, your ladyship!"

He hurried off over the path and disappeared into a small door set in a massive tower. Ravens croaked overhead and fluttered in the floodlights like black confetti. "If the ravens ever leave the Tower of London then the royal family will be destroyed," Gary whispered.

"Is that true?" Pete asked.

"That's the legend," Gary told us. "There are lots of stories about this place. All the people who died here with their heads on the block. Quite a few of them still haunt the place – they say Queen Anne Boleyn walks around with her head tucked underneath her arm!"

"Awwww! That's nice!" Pete said. "I always go to bed like that!"

Gary gasped. "With your head tucked underneath your arm?"

"I'm sorry, Gary," Pete said, blushing. "I thought that you said with her 'ted' tucked underneath her arm!"

I was thinking about ghosts when we stepped through the gateway and saw a terrifying figure move out from the shadow of a doorway.

"Ooooh!" Pete whimpered. "Who's that?"

It was a man. His skinny legs were clothed in black tights and his body in a thick black jacket that was hundreds of years old. He wore a golden crown on his black, shoulder-length hair. But strangest of all was the curious twist of his shoulder and his limp as he moved towards us. "A ghost, perhaps," I hissed.

"Who are you?" Gary asked, his voice trembling.

The man looked at us. "Why, King Richard III, of course! Don't you read your history books?"

"Ooooh! You're dead!" Pete said in a panic. "You must be a ghostie!"

The man sighed. "I'm an actor! My name's Roger Roll. I'm paid to play the part of Richard III," he told us.

"Coo! Was he really that ugly?" Pete asked.

Roger Roll shrugged. "That's the way they want me to play Richard," he said, and pulled a bundle of papers from the front of his jacket. "Look ..."

Richard was ugly from the day he was born. He was born with thick black hair down to his shoulders and a mouth full of teeth! They say his arm was withered and his shoulder hunched. He looked like a monster and he acted like a monster.

John Rous

"John Rous!" Gary exclaimed. "That's the same man that accused Richard of murdering the princes! He really had it in for Uncle Richard, didn't he?"

"Is that true?" I asked the actor.

Roger pulled a cushion out of the back of his jacket and stood up straight. "Probably not. All that was written by his enemies, long after Richard died. But it scares the kids if I limp around and make faces!"

"Do you think he killed the princes?" Gary asked. "That's one of the things we're here to find out."

The actor spread his hands wide. "They reckon the princes died some time in September 1483," he said.

"We know that," Gary said.

"Well, King Richard left London around 20th July and travelled around England to meet his people. There was a plot to rescue the princes in early August – so they must have been alive when he left."

"We know that too," I said.

"He didn't return until nearly Christmas. So, if they died in September then their Uncle Richard couldn't possibly have killed them! He wasn't there at the time!"

"Neither was Mayor Tweed's attacker," Pete put in.

A harsh voice behind us asked suddenly, "What do you kids want?"

We swung round to see a tall Beefeater standing there, fist on one hip and looking angry. In his other fist was a long pole with a sort of axe on the end. I'd seen him on the television and in the Duckpool Daily News. It was Mabel Tweed's Uncle Ricky.

"We've come to investigate Mabel's disappearance," I said.

"And the attack on Mayor Tweed!" Pete added.

"I was here when old Tweed was attacked," he said sharply.

"And you were here when Mabel disappeared. We thought maybe you might know something."

He twisted his face into an ugly sneer then forced it into a smile. "I answered all the police questions!"

"Maybe they didn't ask the right one!" I said, and prodded his red jacket with my finger. "Maybe they should have asked you if you and Mabel slipped over the side of the boat as it sailed past Traitor's Gate! Maybe you let yourself into the Tower through the gate!"

"Why would Mabel do that?" he said, with a short laugh.

"Because you promised her a look at the crown jewels!" I said.

His fist went tighter at his side and I thought he was going to hit me. His jaw was clenched but he managed to say, "Why on earth would I want to hurt poor little Mabel?"

"You want her in your power. When her father dies Mabel will get millions of pounds. Then, if Mabel dies soon after, her mother will get the money... and you can marry her. You're probably planning to do away with *her* then!" I said.

Pete's mouth hung open. Even Gary hadn't worked all this out.

The wicked uncle's eyes were bulging under his bushy brows. "You're just too clever for me. You must be Mabel's Time Detectives. She told me you'd find her and come to rescue her!"

"She did?"

"She did."

"So, where is she?" I asked.

"In the chamber next to the crown jewels," he said. "I'll take you to her now. It's a fair cop, Katie! I give myself up. You're just too clever for me."

He looked at the actor who just stood there holding his hunch. "You'd better come too, Roger." And the Beefeater pointed his pole towards a door into the terrible Tower.

"That's a nasty pole he has in his hand," Gary murmured. "Do you trust him?"

"It's a pike," I said, remembering my history lessons.

"A pike's a fish," Pete said. "I could just fancy some fish and chips."

I sighed. Pete was thinking of his gut again. But I should have listened to the clue in what Pete was saying.

Remember:

Chapter 7
Terror in the Tower

In the days of the little princes the Tower must have been bleak and scary. They must have walked up these stairs and shivered in the dim red light of smoking torches. They must have wondered if they'd ever see daylight again.

But we didn't. Why not? The lights were bright and electric. There were signs telling us just where we were, arrows pointing to the Jewel Room.

But there weren't any signs to tell us the truth...

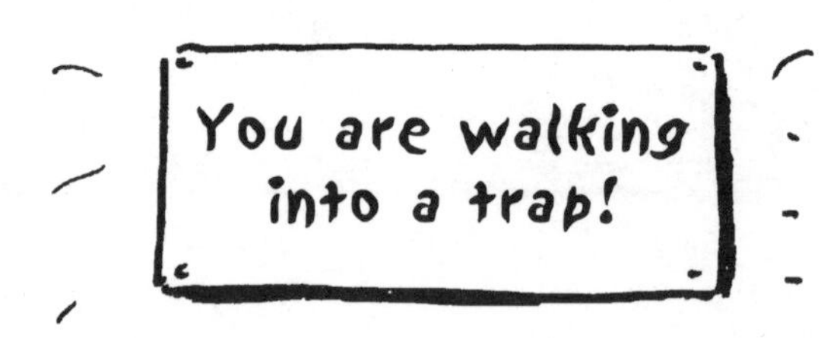

And no sign as we entered the Jewel Room and heard the door slam behind us with a boom like doom...

The gold glittered and the jewels shone like a rainbow inside the brightly lit glass cases.

"Keep going," the Beefeater ordered and we went on to a little door set in the wall. It was a small cupboard with a chair in the middle. A girl sat tied to the chair. She was dressed in a slightly grubby white party dress. Her hair fell in ringlets over her angry red face.

"Mabel! Mabel!" I cried. "We're here! We've rescued you!"

"Do excuse me!" she snapped. "But what has taken you so long?"

"But Mabel..." I began.

"Call yourselves Time Detectives? You couldn't detect a cow in a cowshed!"

"But Mabel..."

"Gary Grint couldn't detect a tree in a forest!"

"But Mabel..."

"You couldn't detect your own scruffy socks on your own scruffy feet, Katie Bucket. And Pete Plank couldn't detect the word detect in a dictionary because he can't even spell. Do excuse me, but do you realise I've been held prisoner here for two days while you miserable detectives have been as much use as a ship without a sail, a dog without a tail or Jack and Jill without a pail!"

She finally ran out of breath. "Sorry, Mabel," Pete muttered miserably.

"No we are NOT sorry!" I exploded. "You... you... ungrateful little pasty-faced prune! You greedy weed Tweed! Face-like-a-table Mabel. You..."

"That's enough," her Uncle Ricky said. "You have ruined my plot to destroy my princess in the Tower. Now I will have to switch to plan number two to make my fortune!"

"Plan number two?" Pete asked. "What's that?"

"Why, to steal the crown jewels, of course!" the man cackled. "I have here the key that switches off the alarm and opens the cases. Outside I have the mayor's Rolls Royce as my getaway car. And I have you lot to take the blame!"

"You'll never get away with it!" Roger Roll the actor cried.

"That's what they said about Richard III," Uncle Ricky snarled, and pointed his pike at the actor. "Now, open the cases and take out the crowns. Load them into this sack!"

Roger's shoulders slumped and he did as he was told. In five minutes the jewel cases were empty and Ricky T Hurd was standing in the doorway with his sack of loot. "Thanks for your help," he laughed. "I'll send nice flowers to your funerals!"

He slammed the door and locked it on the outside. When the echo faded it was as silent as the little princes' graves in there. I hammered on the door but it only hurt my hand.

"What do we do?" Pete wailed.

"Do excuse me," Mabel said. "But the first thing you can do is set me free!"

I looked at Gary. "I suppose we have to."

"I suppose so," he agreed, and we unfastened her from the chair.

"Now we just have to wait to be released in the morning," she said. "That dreadful uncle was right. He's going to get away with it, just like Richard III."

"But Richard didn't really get away with it, did he?" Roger Roll the actor asked.

"Didn't he?" I asked. "We haven't found any proof that he murdered the princes."

"He didn't," Roger said, tugging at the scripts under his costume and pulling them out. "At least he didn't do it himself. But he did order someone else to do it. And that man confessed years later!"

Show us!" I said eagerly. "We worked out when the princes must have died. But we still don't know how they died or who killed them. I guess it will pass the time till we're set free."

Roger unrolled a sheet and we studied it.

THE RICHARD III STORY

Actor's notes

Page 1

Lots of people will come to the Tower and ask about the disappearance of the little princes. Some people are quite sure that Richard III was guilty – other people are just as sure he had nothing to do with it. Try to be fair.

You can say Richard III was not in London at the time the princes probably died. But, of course, he could have sent someone else to do the deed.

Almost thirty years after Richard III died, a man called Thomas More wrote a history of Richard III. Thomas More was only six at the time when the Princes in the Tower disappeared. So how did he get the story? He said…

> "I shall tell you of the sad end of those babes. I will not repeat all the stories I have heard. I shall tell you the men and the methods that are most likely to be true."

I sank onto the stone floor and the others sat beside me – except Mabel who stayed on her chair. It was getting warm in the little room and I was feeling tired.

"So there's a story about the end of the princes, but it could be a lie?" Gary asked.

"That's right!" Roger Roll said. "And it's much too frightening to tell youngsters like you!" he went on.

"Roger," I yawned. "We've come all this way to find the truth and if you don't tell us the answer I will use Ricky T Hurd's pike to tickle your tonsils. So spill the beans!"

"I wish I had a plate of beans," Pete said. "With me fish and chips."

We ignored him. Roger showed us the copy of the ancient document written just thirty years after the princes vanished. He was right. It's gruesome. If you're a wimp or a vegetarian then skip this bit...

Thomas More's tale

King Richard III was touring England to meet his people while the Princes Edward and Dickon were left in the Tower of London. One day he sent his servant, John Green, to the keeper of the Tower, Sir Robert Brackenbury, and ordered him to murder the princes.

Sir Robert replied, "I would never put them to death, even if it costs me my own life."

When Richard III heard this in his bedroom he complained, "Will no-one do me this service?"

One of Richard III's servants said he knew where there was the right man for this job – a knight called Sir James Tyrell. "This Tyrell would do anything to please Your Majesty," the servant said.

So Richard sent for Tyrell and gave him a letter. The letter was to Sir Robert Brackenbury. It ordered the keeper of the Tower to hand over the keys to Tyrell for just one night.

Now Tyrell rode back to London and gave the letter to Brackenbury. That very night he was left in the Tower with the princes and their jailer, a murderer called Miles Forest. Tyrell also had his own horse-keeper, a big, broad, strong villain called John Dighton.

When the Tower was deserted, about midnight, these two men came to the chamber where the helpless children lay asleep. They entered the cell and wrapped them up in their bedclothes. They wrapped them so tightly, keeping down by force the feather bed and pillows hard into their mouths. Within a while, smothered and stifled, their breath failing, they gave up to God their innocent souls and went to the joys of heaven. They left to their tormentors their bodies, dead in the bed. After the villains saw them to be thoroughly dead, they laid their bodies naked on the bed and fetched Sir James Tyrell to see them.

On seeing them he ordered the murderers to bury them at the foot of the stairs, deep in the ground, under a pile of stones.

Even in the heat of the Jewel Room we shivered.

"Horrible," Gary whispered. "At least they probably never knew what happened. They just went to sleep and never woke up."

"And just how we are going to end up," I told him.

Pete blinked and tried to stay awake. "You mean Ricky T Hurd will come back when we fall asleep and smother us?"

"No. I mean the air in here is choking," I told him. "I think they've built this room air-tight like a bank safe. Once we've breathed all the oxygen we'll drop off to sleep and never wake up!"

"Ricky T Hurd didn't know that," Gary groaned.

"I think he did," I said. "He knew that after a night in here we wouldn't be around in the morning to be witnesses. That's what he meant when he said, 'I'll send nice flowers to your funerals!'"

"Uhh?" Pete grunted. "I hope he sends dandelions. "I like dandelions."

Chapter 8
Air today and gone tomorrow

"At least we're nice and warm," Pete said cheerfully after an hour, when the air in the little room had become hot and stale.

Five minutes later it was hotter and staler. "Katie?" Pete went on cheerfully. "Where do we go when we die?"

Mabel cut in, "Ask your brain, Pete Plank... it's been dead for years."

The room was dim, just a single light in the ceiling. And the empty jewel cases glowing a faint red. We'd sunk to the floor to wait for the air to run out. "Maybe we'll get to meet the two princes!" Roger Roll said gloomily.

"Yeah," I sighed. "Then we find out what really happened to them."

"But their Uncle Richard had them suffocated and buried under the stairs at the Tower," Gary said.

"Nah! Someone would have found them sooner or later," I argued.

"Oh, but they did!" Roger Roll said.

"What?" I cried. "The princes really were killed and buried here? I thought it was all a mystery. That's what we've been trying to detect!" I groaned. "We got ourselves killed for nothing."

"Not nothing," Pete said. "We rescued Mabel!" he grinned.

Mabel looked at him with eyes that were like deadly nightshade. "Do excuse me, but if this is being rescued I'd have been better off without it."

"Stop all this arguing," I said. "You're wasting air." I turned to the actor. "So tell us about finding the bodies of the princes."

He pulled his notes from his jacket and searched through them. "This is what I have to tell the visitors when I act the part of the wicked Uncle Richard," he said. He cleared his throat, rose to his feet and gave the performance of his life. I guess it was going to be the last performance of his life so he wanted to make a good job of it!

Ah! The White Tower! A place of blood and misery. But a hundred and ninety years after the miserable little princes disappeared parts had become ruined. King Charles II pulled down some buildings and here, at a corner of the Tower, the workmen uncovered a stairway.
My tortured spirit screamed at them to stop! They didn't hear me! They dug down under the bottom stair. Aieeee! At a depth of three metres they uncovered a wooden chest! And – when they opened it – they found...

The skeletons of two children – the taller one on its back, the smaller one on top of it, face down! King Charles decided after four years that these were the bones of my little princes and he had them buried in Westminster Abbey. But were they allowed to rest in peace?
No!! For in 1933 the little skeletons were dug up and examined by scientists. They announced that one child was about 12 years old and one was about 10... The ages of the princes when I was supposed to have murdered them! So, of course I got the blame! What can I say? Just this...

Roger sank down exhausted onto the floor of the Jewel Room. "That's how they'll find us, five hundred years from now!" Mabel wailed and wasted more good air – my air!

"Mabel. They will find us tomorrow morning when they open up! And just like the princes no-one will know who did it, that's the annoying thing!" I said wearily.

"Do excuse me! But I have no wish to see that dreadful Ricky T Hurd get away with this!" Mabel said. "I will leave a note!"

Suddenly we all brightened up at the idea. "And I can leave a note for my mum!" Gary said. "If I'm late home for my tea cos I'm dead then she'll kill me!"

"Uhh?" Pete asked, and for once I agreed with him.

Mabel began…

Dear friend,
We want you to know that it wasn't an accident that we were locked in here. A man called Ricky T Hurd kidnapped me and planned to kill me. When my Time Detectives team found me and spoiled his plan he locked us in here and ran off with a sackful of jewels. We hope you catch him and use some of the Tower's really nasty torture instruments on him to pull his ugly nose off.
Tell Daddy I hope his head gets better soon and that Ricky is to blame for that too.

Signed
Mabel Tweed
(Millionaire mayor's daughter)

Luckily she left the other side of the paper for us to scribble notes…

Dear Mum,
Sorry I missed my tea but I couldn't help it. Don't forget to feed the hamster for me. Give my computer to my little sister and my violin to the school orchestra and my train-spotting book to Duckpool museum.
Your loving son, Gary

Dear Mum and Dad,
Don't cry. I went the way I wanted to go – on the trail of a vile villain. Have my football boots stuffed and put in a glass case if you want to remember me.
Katie

Yes. All right. I know it's not the world's best dying message – but you try doing better!

There was enough room for Pete to add a message on the bottom. He shrugged. "I'm not much good at writing, Katie," he said. "I've been thinking..."

"Hah!" Mabel Tweed exploded. "Thinking! That must have been the ticking noise I could hear. I thought we were locked up in here with a time bomb!"

I turned on her and used precious air to say, "Mabel Tweed, if you insult my friend Pete Plank again, then I'll save one-fifth of the air in here by smothering you myself! Will you shut up, you vicious little madam!"

Her look this time was even deadlier than deadly nightshade but she didn't dare to say anything else. I turned back to Pete. "Sorry, Pete, what were you thinking?"

"I thought... don't laugh, Katie..."

"I won't laugh, Pete."

"I thought I might give my message to one of those meat-eaters out there. Save me having to write it down," he said.

"It's Beefeaters you..." Mabel began. I looked at her. She stopped.

I rested a hand on Pete's arm. "Yes, Pete, that's a very good idea," I said gently. "But have you thought about how we can get a message to the Beefeaters outside when we're locked in here?"

Pete gave a wide, simple smile. "Of course I've thought of that Katie! I'm not stupid, you know!"

Mabel's mouth opened. Then it snapped shut.

"I know you're not stupid, Pete. So, how we can get a message to the Beefeaters outside?" I asked.

"You see that jewel case, Katie?" he asked.

"Yes, Pete."

"You see that red glow?"

"Yes, Pete."

"Well that's cos of the magic red beams that run across it. If a burglar sticks his hand in the case it sets off an alarm," he said shyly. In that steaming room I went cold at the thought.

Pete couldn't be right. He couldn't. It was too much to hope for.

"Don't laugh, Katie," he said. (The truth is, I was almost crying.) "Don't laugh – but I thought if we break the glass, the meat-eaters would come and open up to see what's happening. We could give them our messages before we suffocate! Is that a daft idea Katie, is it?"

Mabel's jaw was hanging open. Gary looked at him the way he looks at a diesel train in Duckpool station and Roger Roll looked as if he'd been given a star part in a Hollywood film.

I rose to my feet, took off my shoe and held it over the empty glass case. I could see the red, hair-line beams inside the case.

I raised the shoe over my head and brought the heel down as hard as I could on the glass.

The shoe bounced off the glass and smacked me on the nose.

Chapter 9

The king with no crown and no clothes

Mabel Tweed clapped her hands. Very slowly. "Do excuse me, but aren't you supposed to break the glass and not your nose?"

I'd love to have broken about 206 of Mabel's bones but I stayed calm. "We need something hard and heavy."

"Pete Plank's brain?" Mabel suggested.

I stayed calm. Roger Roll, Gary and Pete began to peer into the darkened corners of the room. It was Roger who said, "The Beefeater's pike! He had to leave it behind so he could carry his loot away!"

He brought the heavy weapon into the middle of the room. I was almost afraid to watch. If this didn't work then we really were finished. Pete's idea had raised our hopes. It was going to be really cruel if we were beaten now.

"Maybe I can test it on Mabel's head?" I suggested.

She stuck her tongue out at me.

We stood back to give Roger Roll room. He raised the long pole as high as he could under the curved stone room and swung it down hard.

There was a sharp crack. The glass had cracked but the pike hadn't broken through. He turned the head round so the point of the pike was chipping at the tough glass. Little pieces of glass fell inside the case and the red beams went out.

"Ooooh!" Pete breathed. "I think you broke it, Roger."

The actor sat down, tired and out of breath, on the floor. "Well, that's it. If there are alarm bells ringing somewhere we'll just have to wait and see."

We waited. I decided to take my team's mind off our problems and asked Roger, "So Uncle Richard probably killed the princes?"

He shrugged. "There is another suspect. Some people think that the princes lived quietly here for two years. It was the next king, Henry VII, who found them and had them murdered."

"Uhh?" Pete frowned. "You mean that King Richard only lasted two years?"

"That's right! There was a Welshman, Henry Tudor, who said the crown should be his," Roger said eagerly. "He was living in France when Richard was crowned. But, two years later, he gathered an army and landed in Wales. Richard marched out to meet him and they met on a battlefield called Bosworth Field, near Leicester."

"I thought this Richard III was a great fighter," Gary argued.

"He was – but I was betrayed!" Roger cried. He gave a foolish smile. "I mean Richard was betrayed. Look, we do this mock newspaper for tourists to tell the story."

He handed us a crumpled copy...

The Bosworth Times

Still only one groat

22 August 1485

King Richard betrayed and beaten

Henry Tudor crowned on Bosworth Battlefield

Richard III is dead. The ex-king met his match when he went into battle with Henry Tudor at Bosworth today. The Welsh Wizard Tudor became King Henry VII when he was crowned after the battle. The rumour is that the crown was found hanging from a thorn bush.

I watched the battle from Richard's camp on top of Ambien Hill. I had a quick interview with his ex-highness shortly after breakfast. "I feel a bit rough," he admitted. "I had a bad night – dreadful dreams where I was surrounded by demons. But I'm fighting fit now and I know my men will smash that terrible Tudor!"

From his high ground on Ambien Hill King Richard watched as the Tudor troops battled their way up and were hacked back down by the Duke of Norfolk's troops. Henry Tudor was keeping well back from the fight and from our camp we could see his banner flapping with the red dragon of Wales.

They could see Richard just as clearly with his golden crown on top of his armoured helmet.

Richard had to be favourite to win, but the big worry was Lord Stanley. His lordship had promised to fight for Richard, but he held his men to one side and refused to join in. Then the brave Duke of Norfolk was hacked down and King Richard really lost his cool. Climbing onto his white horse he led a furious charge down the hill, desperate to carve a way through to Henry Tudor and knock him down.

That's when Lord Stanley joined the battle – on Henry Tudor's side! His men smashed into the side of Richard's charging knights. Richard himself was dragged down off his horse by Welsh pikemen and hacked to death on the ground, battling to the last.

The body was stripped and thrown across a horse. There are no plans to hold a funeral. Tonight Henry Tudor is heading for London and the throne of England.

The king is dead – long live the king! ♛

"He died with no clothes on – just like the princes," I said.

"Poor old Richard," Pete said.

"Poor old Richard!" Mabel squawked. "He probably killed two kids, our age, just a few yards from here! I'm glad they got him. And I hope they get Ricky T Hurd just the same!"

"What? Knock him off his horse, take his clothes off and throw him on a horse again?" Pete frowned.

I waited for Mabel's cruel reply. There was a silence and then a sudden snore. Mabel had fallen asleep.

Gary said, "Mabel? Mabel?"

Mabel snored.

"It's only seven o'clock," Pete said. "She must go to bed early!"

Roger shook her shoulder and then patted her cheek. Mabel didn't wake. He turned towards us. "It's the lack of oxygen," he explained. "She won't wake up – ever – if she doesn't get some oxygen soon," the actor said. He yawned and slumped beside her.

Pete's chin was on his chest and Gary's eyes had a dreamy, faraway look. I felt pretty dizzy myself. I sat on the floor and stared at the door. It was like a massive safe with a huge wheel in the middle.

Have you ever spun around until you're dizzy? When you stop it feels as if the rest of the world is moving. That's how I began to feel.

I fixed my eyes on the wheel in the door. Something that wouldn't move and make me feel so sick. For just a few seconds it worked... but, as my eyes began to close, even that wheel seemed to be spinning... spinning... spinning...

Chapter 10
The truth about the Tower

Of course, when I imagined the wheel turning I only imagined I was imagining it, because I didn't imagine it and it really was turning. See?

The door swung open. Our lives had been saved thanks to Plank. The last thing I remember seeing was the face of a baffled Beefeater. Then I passed out and woke up in hospital.

The *Duckpool Daily News* told the story the next day...

The Duckpool Daily News

5 January

55p

MILLIONAIRE MABEL FREE

Kruel kidnapper kaptured

Missing millionaire Mabel Tweed was found last night – in the Tower of London, where her wicked uncle, Ricky T Hurd, worked as a Beefeater. Today Mabel is recovering in the same hospital as her famous father, Mayor Walter Tweed, who was suffering from a cracked nut. Police believe the Beefeater's to blame for the bash that brained him.

After the Town Hall attack Mayor Tweed called for his Rolls Royce to take him home from hospital. The loyal driver arrived at the hospital where a policeman spotted a Beefeater with a bag in the back of the car. "The deranged driver

The tearful reunion at Mabel Tweed's bedside last night

wouldn't let me out!" the Beefeater bellowed. "The dope was supposed to take me to the airport, but the mayor's message came through and he drove to Duckpool instead. Kept saying something about, 'I speed to the needs of Tweed!' He's potty! He shouldn't be allowed on the road! And I haven't stolen these crown jewels... I was just taking them home to give them a bit of a polish." He then threw them in the hospital gutter and said, "Anyway, those aren't my jewels, I've never seen them before in my life."

Chief Inspector Norse

Chief Inspector Norse said, "We think he may be telling a bit of a fib. He will be arrested for kidnapping Mabel Tweed, attempting to murder the mayor, stealing the crown jewels and dropping litter in a hospital gutter. He should get about 99 years in prison."

Meanwhile, inside the hospital the brave little Mabel made a statement. "My dear friends, Katie Bucket and the Time Detectives, tracked me to the Tower. Alas they were trapped by the kidnapper and almost suffocated to death like the little princes! Luckily my quick thinking saved our lives and saved the crown jewels! I don't expect a medal, of course – well, not a very large one – just a small one would do." Mayor Tweed is at this moment arranging to have one made.

Our reporter asked Miss Tweed who she thought was to blame for imprisoning the children and trying to suffocate them. "I think it was probably King Richard III," she said. The young heroine's brain is clearly suffering from her terror in the Tower.

Next week we were back in the classroom and Miss Toon was very upset that our Time Detecting had got us into so much trouble.

"You could have been dead!" she said.

"Not as dead as the two princes," I said.

"And did you work out what happened to them?" she asked.

"One day someone will be able to prove if those bones really belonged to the princes. If they do, then the princes died aged 10 and 12 – and those were their ages when Richard III took the throne. That could prove him guilty once and for all," I said and handed her our report...

So the Time Detectives failed to solve the case ... but people have been trying for five hundred years and done no better.

Little Prince Edward was never crowned... but hopefully Mabel Tweed will be crowned next week. She gets her medal – the medal that really belongs to poor Pete Plank.

Mabel will be sitting in the mayor's chair – just underneath the crystal chandelier. I've got my pet rat trained and ready... well, OK, actually it's my hamster.

The Time Detectives have been invited to watch, and to be honest, we can't wait to see Mabel crowned!!! (Nah! Only joking. Our real revenge will be complete when she sits on the whoopee cushion! (Heh! Heh! Heh!)

WHOOPEE!

Time trail

1483

9 April King Edward IV dies and leaves a wife, five daughters and two sons. The older son, Edward Prince of Wales aged 12, will become the next king. If the Prince of Wales dies then the younger son, Dickon aged 10, will become king. That's as clear as the nose on your face.

30 April Prince Edward was living in Wales when his dad died. Now he rides towards London to be crowned. His uncle, Anthony Rivers, has been looking after him in Wales and probably expects to look after the prince till he is old enough to rule for himself. That's the job of "Protector". But on this day they arrive at Stony Stratford where they meet the dead king's brother, Uncle Richard, the Duke of Gloucester. Uncle Richard has Uncle Anthony arrested and locked away. Uncle Richard takes charge of Prince Edward.

10 May The government decides Prince Edward needs a "Protector" and gives the job to Uncle Richard. Surprise, surprise! They also set the date of Prince Edward's coronation for 24 June. But will it ever happen?

10 June Uncle Richard says Prince Edward's mother, Queen Elizabeth, is plotting against him. He sends for his army in the north to join him in London.

16 June When Uncle Richard's army arrives he surrounds the palace of Queen Elizabeth and forces her to give up her younger son, Prince Dickon. Now Uncle Richard has BOTH princes and he sends them to the Tower of London to 'protect' them. (Ho! Ho! Believe that if you like!) The coronation is cancelled.

22 June Instead of a coronation there is a church service at St Paul's Cross. The priest announces that dead King Edward had a wife before he married Queen Elizabeth – so he couldn't have married Elizabeth properly and neither of the two princes can be king! Who can they give the job to?

26 June The lords and knights decide to ask Uncle Richard to be their next king – Richard III. Uncle Richard accepts the job.

6 July Richard is crowned king... while the two poor princes are left to rot in the Tower of London.

20 July King Richard III sets off on a tour of his country to meet the people. The princes are not invited. Richard III leaves London and soon after there is an attempt to rescue the princes from the Tower. The rescue fails and the plotters are punished.

8 September Richard III makes his own son the Prince of Wales. It seems Prince Edward has lost the job as well as losing the crown – or is he already dead?

1485

August Richard III meets Henry Tudor at the Battle of Bosworth Field. Henry hammers him and heads for London. It is just possible that the princes are still alive and living in the Tower. If so, then Henry Tudor has them murdered.